Wings For Soaring

Taking It To The Next Level
Beyond Jonathan Livingston Seagull

An Uplifting Novella
Exploring Life's Ultimate Questions & Concerns

By Psychologist/Pilot

"Dr. Dan" Matzke, PhD

Wings For Soaring - Seventh Edition

Cover Photo Credit: Bald Eagle Image by Softeis

For information about other books and programs by Dr. Dan visit: *UpliftingPerspectives.net*

About "Dr. Dan": Dan Matzke, a.k.a. "Dr. Dan", holds a Ph.D. in psychology. Dr. Dan worked as a licensed Psychologist and Marriage & Family Therapist for over 25 years. He taught psychology classes and did consulting work (testing & evaluations), prior to retiring from private practice in California and moving to Jackson Hole, Wyoming. He now enjoys writing and mentoring, when not hiking, fishing, skiing, traveling or flying. Dr. Dan has a commercial pilot's license, with flight instructor ratings for airplanes and gliders. He is a winner of the highly prized Barron Hilton Soaring Cup.

Historical Note: This story was originally written as a sequel to *Jonathan Livingston Seagull* by Richard Bach. However, the publisher and author would not sanction a sequel, and forbid the use of the character names. To avoid copyright infringement and litigation, the names of the characters and parts of the story line were changed in the present version.

Philosophical Note: This story explores what might best be called "real-life intelligence" or "existential savvy". It goes beyond the basics of "pop psychology" and "emotional intelligence"… to the next level… which entails coming to terms with life & living. These are fundamental questions and concerns which humans have wrestled with throughout all of recorded history. Confronting these issues can be rather anxiety-provoking and disquieting, and it usually requires a relatively high level of emotional intelligence to even start the process. Ultimately, however, recognizing and resolving these matters can be very liberating and empowering, freeing a person to function more effectively, to thrive and to prosper.

Acknowledgement Note: Ideas for this story were drawn from many contemporary writers, who have in turn drawn from seminal thinkers and authors throughout history. Interested readers are referred to the books (& songs) of Irvin D. Yalom, Robert C. Solomon, Carl Rogers, Rollo May, Abraham Maslow, Viktor Frankl, John Denver, and Richard Bach.

Dedication Note: To my wife and life partner – Julie. Thanks for all of your support. It has been a *grand adventure...*

Wings for Soaring – Introduction

It had been many flight-years since Elliot had become an outcast from the Rocky Mountain Council of Eagles. He remembered as if it were yesterday, the feelings of bitterness, anger and revenge he first felt. Expelled from the society not for reckless flying or defiant-daredevil stunts, but for the persistent pelting of chief elders with disquieting questions. "Why not?" questions, "What for?" questions, "Who says?" questions, and the like. Then he met Ezekiel. This was a bird who could understand Elliot's passion to question and to learn.

Elliot learned a great deal about flying, and about the nature of being an eagle, from "Zeek" (Ezekiel's flight call sign). Most of all he acquired a joy of learning, and developed a desire to continue growing, and to question limits.

After Zeek left, Elliot became the Chief Instructor, working with other outcast birds that were eager to learn about forbidden realms of flight. The more he instructed, the more he learned about the subtleties of soaring, and of being an eagle. He remembered a saying from an ancient elder, "To teach is to learn," and the more he taught, the more he learned indeed.

Many stories and myths spread about Zeek after he left. Some spoke of him as being the son of the Exalted Eagle, with magical, supernatural powers. Many elders still spoke of him as being a devil, out to destroy the gaggle. Try as he might Elliot could not convince them otherwise.

Elliot had come to see that Zeek was indeed a unique bird, unique both in his desire to learn, and to share his understanding with others. However, Elliot was perplexed by Zeek's ideas about limits. In all of his instruction, Zeek kept emphasizing "no limits". That "if we break the chains of our thought, we can break the chains of our body too." And "the role of a teacher is to help others break out of their limits."

To a large extent, Elliot found this to be true. Many of the limits he had tested he found to be self-imposed, or imposed by the law of the flock. In reality these limits were self-defeating and sabotaging. Because they appeared to limit one's freedom, they did.

Elliot had found a great deal of satisfaction in testing these synthetic limits, and breaking free of the myths and illusions of the flock. However, he continued to wrestle with Zeek's assertion of "no limits". Could it be, he wondered, that there are some hard and fast limits which cannot be exceeded or overcome? Could there be some "givens", which an eagle could spend a lifetime trying to overcome or beat, all to no avail? Would this not be a futile waste of time and energy, trying to break through these absolute limits? If such limits do exist, would it not be wise to accept these "givens", to surrender to them gracefully, and enjoy the vast freedom a bird has within these limits?

For example, Elliot had experienced a block in how close he could get to a fellow bird. No matter how well he knew another eagle, no matter how much they flew together or talked, there always seemed to be a gap or space between them. This sense of separateness was profound at times, resulting in Elliot feeling isolated not only from others, but also from the world around him, and even parts of himself. He wondered if this apartness could be a limit-form?

Elliot also had experienced a dilemma in choices and commitments. Many times he found that he had wanted to do more than one thing at a given time, but found it impossible. Could this be another confine which can not be overcome?

Elliot was also troubled at times over changes and endings. He experienced a continual process of change in life, a process of growth and development which he liked. However, at times he also longed for permanence and stability, which he was not able to find. Could it be that this too is another given, he wondered, a limit-form which is unconquerable?

On many occasions Elliot had pondered the meaning and purpose of life. He had read the works of many great elder eagles, studying their philosophical and religious teachings. Yet he found that he had many questions which were unanswered. He wondered if it could be that there is a limit to our understanding and knowledge. Could there be questions without answers?

These matters troubled Elliot. He had learned to enjoy the process of questioning limits, and had found that most limits were just mental structures, which birds used to quell their anxieties and fears in flight.

But could there be some real absolute limits, some edges to experience, beyond which even an eagle cannot pass? The possibility was intriguing, and Elliot wanted to know.

And so it was that Elliot decided to take a sabbatical from his Chief Instructor position, and to seek some answers to questions on limits.

Wings for Soaring - Part I

Elliot thought he would begin his quest by comparing notes with Elizabeth, a friend and fellow instructor, who was also a friend of Zeek's.

He had come to know Elizabeth when they both worked at a special clinic for O/C (Out-of-Control) eagles. Many of the patients in the clinic had become addicted to "speed". Their relentless pursuit of flying faster and faster had resulted in their lives getting so out of balance that many of them had become mere bone and feather, forsaking friends and food. Others had become hooked on daredevilry and risk-taking. By exceeding the limits of their skill and understanding many had nearly killed themselves and others.

Through their work and by sharing in the joys and disappointments of trying to help O/C birds, Elliot and Elizabeth had become very close. Elliot had heard that Elizabeth had gone on to study love and intimacy, and he thought that perhaps she would have some insight into the nature of closeness and apartness. There he would begin his search for an understanding of the nature of limits.

Elliot left Jackson Hole and headed west to meet with Elizabeth at the Teton Valley roost, a special training school for fledging eagles on the west side of the Teton Mountain range. Besides being a beautiful place to fly and talk, a former student, Eleanor, had an eatery there which served delicious home-made fish soup.

Elliot and Elizabeth rendezvoused over Cascade Canyon west of Inspiration Point and soared together for several hours, thermaling up to 14,000 feet over the Grand Tetons, Schoolroom Glacier and Snowdrift Lake, doing a few formation wing-overs, chandelles, and lazy-eights. It felt good to experience the joy of soaring with an old friend, and it renewed the bond of their friendship.

"I'm on a sabbatical", said Elliot, "a quest of sorts, to try to understand more about limits."

Elizabeth was intrigued by Elliot's use of the word "limits", for she remembered Zeek's passion with it.

"What is it that you are trying to understand?" asked Elizabeth, eager to hear about Elliot's quest.

"Well," Elliot began, "as you know, I have done many things over the years which questioned limits, physical, mental, and flock limits, in an effort to see as clearly as possible, the true nature of an eagle's being. Our friend, Zeek, inspired my search many flight-years ago, and I remember well his repeatedly saying 'No Limits!'. And for the most part, I have enjoyed sharing with others the freedoms I have come to learn. In my naive enthusiasm, I assumed for a long time that all limits could be overcome, if only I worked at it long and hard enough. Ever so slowly, however, I have come to question this assumption. There have been several experiences which I've had which suggest that there may be some 'givens', some absolute limits which cannot be totally overcome. This possibility has so captured me, that I've decided to confront it directly, to learn all that I can about the nature of limits".

"How may I be of help?" Elizabeth asked, sensing that her friend had a question for her.

"It's about the limits of closeness and separateness", Elliot said, quietly. "No matter how close I have gotten to you, or other birds, I have always felt as if there was a gap between us. There is always a sense of separateness and apartness, which I've never been able to completely overcome. I have come to think that there may be a limit as to how close two can become. I have also experienced this sense of being 'a part of, yet apart from', in relation to parts of myself and my surroundings. I have wondered whether or not I am alone in my struggling with these things, and I would like to hear of your experiences and understanding".

"As I see it, Elliot", Elizabeth began, "we all enter life alone, and we depart, or die, alone. Anxiety, tension, and conflict result from our awareness of our absolute aloneness, and we often wish for contact, protection, and to be part of a larger whole, such as the flock. No matter how close each of us becomes to another, there always remains a final unbridgeable gap, a separateness between us.

"There are three forms of separateness and isolation which bird-beings commonly experience", Elizabeth went on to explain. "One is interpersonal aloneness, a sense of loneliness or social isolation. This has been aggravated by the decline of several aspects of eagle culture and lifestyle. One is the decrease in family involvement. Oftentimes extended family members are several thousand miles apart, spread out and very separate. Eagle councils have also become more and more isolated, with less of an eagle-hood feeling. Gatherings and flock functions have also declined over the past few generations. These decreases in bird interaction over the years have heightened the sense of aloneness.

"A second type of isolation, Elliot, is separation within. This often results from splits between our body, mind and emotions. An example might be a split in which one does not trust his own intuition, or his own judgment.

"It can involve being out of touch with one's own body. The mind may be moving along at warp speed, and not be honoring or respecting some of the physical needs for food or rest. Other splits occur because of accepting as absolute, some of the flock's shoulds and oughts, that we were programmed with early in life, over one's own feelings, intuition, or preferences.

"A third form of apart-from-ness is worldly estrangement. This refers to a sense of separation between one's self and the world, a feeling that you are not a part of it all, that you do not fit. A phrase that captures it is that 'you are in this world, but not of this world'. There is a sense of strangeness, of not being at home, of being alien to the eagle fellowship.

"To temper this sense of aloneness and separateness, a bird can use the world as a tool, by engaging in life fully. Constructive ways through which we can cope with this sense of isolation can be found. One way of dealing with this condition is through creative activity. This results in a union of the artist with the medium, a way of bridging the separateness. Soaring flight, for example, often results in a sense of oneness with the environment. The ancient Zen eagles spoke of a union of form and flight, in which it's impossible to tell where one's flight feathers end, and flight begins.

"Another way in which we can temper aloneness is through membership, whether you are a member of the council, or of the outcasts. Becoming a part of a group, helps moderate the feelings of aloneness and separateness.

"A third way of handling this given is through meditation or vigorous activities, such as aerobatic flight, which can result in new vistas in which a bird experiences a sense of harmony and accord."

"And what about love?" asked Elliot.

"Love", replied Elizabeth, "is perhaps one of the most satisfying ways of dealing with aloneness and isolation, where two individuals become one in a relationship, experiencing a sense of closeness and intimacy.

"Relationships cannot eliminate isolation, yet aloneness can be shared. Love compensates for the pain of separateness. Relationships can provide a bridge from one alone self to another alone self.

"There is however," cautioned Elizabeth," a dilemma that we encounter in relationships, the dilemma of fusion versus isolation. Fusion, to leech or cling to, versus isolation, to be apart and alone. This is a major developmental task; to relate to others without using them only as a tool for reducing the anxiety of isolation.

"As I understand it, Elliot, we need to accept the basic given of aloneness and separateness as a limit-form that cannot be totally overcome. If not, we may seek desperately to avoid or deny it. This can result in many self-defeating and destructive behaviors. One form is through developing dependent or manipulative relationships. This type of relationship, in which a bird is desperately clinging to another, clutching to them, trying to overcome the sense of aloneness, usually tends to alienate the other, driving them away, which in turn aggravates the aloneness and isolation felt originally.

"Another wanton way of trying to avoid this given is through eating fermented berries or mushrooms, to obtain chemically induced sensations of bliss and harmony.

"Through facing and accepting aloneness and separateness as a given of bird-being existence," Elizabeth concluded, "we, in effect, reduce our anxiety and tension, and thereby are less likely to engage in sabotaging actions, in a desperate attempt to avoid or overcome this basic limit-form."

Elliot pondered Elizabeth's words, recognizing the wisdom in what she said. Her account echoed his experiences, and hearing it helped him to understand more clearly the nature of this limit-form. There was something about hearing a friend put into words what he had experienced and knew intuitively, that resulted in a sense of acceptance of this given. Indeed, by confronting and facing this issue head-on, it became clear to Elliot that no matter how close he became to another, he would still face life alone. This was a limit, an edge to eagle-existence, which could not be exceeded.

Elliot thanked Elizabeth for sharing her understanding, and after finishing a second helping of Eleanor's trout soup at the Teton Valley roost, he prepared to depart.

"What's next?" asked Elizabeth, sensing Elliot's eagerness to continue with his quest.

"I'm going to look up Zeek." replied Elliot. "I promised him that I would appear on his flight plan someday, and the time is now. I hear he's working with the Northwestern Counsel, developing an advanced training program for cross-country flights."

"Zeek, working with the counsel?" Elizabeth questioned, with a surprised look.

"Yea, I know." said Elliot with a grin on his face. "Sounds like Zeek's years of practicing patience and compassion paid off."

After a farewell hug, Elliot lifted off and headed north, to talk with another old friend who knew of limits.

Wings for Soaring - Part II

As Elliot flew over the high plateau near Old Faithful geyser, he caught a boomer thermal and climbed at 1000 feet-per-minute to cloud base at 17,000 feet above sea level. From that altitude he could make a straight glide to the West Yellowstone perch. At about one mile out, Elliot pulled in his wings, leaving just the tips of his flight feathers extended, and dove to 217 m.p.h. As he passed over the threshold he pulled straight up and did a 16 point roll, stopping crisply at each point. At the top as his speed bled off, he completed a hammer-head turn, and dove straight down toward the landing area, keeping his speed slow by twisting his flight feathers to form giant dive brakes. At about twenty feet he began his round-out, and made a tip-toe, no-step landing right next to a group of elders.

"Hello Elliot!!" said Zeek, delighted to see an old student and friend. "I thought that might be you, although I like how you concluded your fly-by better today than the first time, when you tried to fly through granite."

"Hi, Zeek. Thanks for noticing the improvements in my routine," Elliot replied with a smile.

The elders looked at Elliot with some disdain, but seemed to tolerate him since he was a friend of Zeek's.

Zeek finished up the work he was doing for the day, and the two flew out over Mammoth Hot Springs to catch up on many years of time-flight. On the way not a word was spoken. A formation flight of graceful aerial ballet transpired, which reflected the joy these two birds experienced flying together again.

"You've learned much, Elliot." commented Zeek after they had landed in a tall pine tree overlooking the Yellowstone area. "You have shed many limits since we last flew together."

"It's about limits that I have come to talk with you, Zeek." Elliot said rather abruptly. "I'm curious to know if you have encountered any limit-forms which you have found to be authentic, or are they all just illusions of a bird's mind?"

Zeek started right in, as if no time had passed since they had last spoken together. "Well, Elliot, I have continued to learn and to develop my thinking over the years. When we last spoke, I truly believed that there were no limits which could not be surmounted. However, with age and wisdom, I have come to a viewpoint of limits which can be summarized by two general statements: Alternatives Exclude, and Everything Fades."

Elliot was both shocked and relieved to hear Zeek acknowledge the existence of limits. He thought for a moment....

Alternatives Exclude.... Everything Fades. "Rather harsh sounding," he thought out loud.

"Yes." said Zeek softly.

"I want to know more." said Elliot. "Tell me about these limits you have come to know."

"OK." said Zeek, as he prepared to speak at length by fluffing his flight feathers and settling on his perch in the tall pine.

"The first limit I've come to understand actually deals with freedom and responsibility. Freedom refers to the absence of external structure, a lack of restrictions or laws. Eagles have literal freedom to author their own life design, their choices and commitments. This freedom results in anxiety from the realization that with freedom comes responsibility. If I have the freedom to choose what I shall do, then I am accountable for whatever I choose to do, or choose not to do.

"To deal with this awesome, anxiety-provoking condition, bird-beings tend to seek structure, to seek out guidelines and rules of authority, as a way of shielding themselves from absolute freedom. This is done in an attempt to avoid the reality that there are no universal imperatives in life; no absolute shoulds, oughts or musts.

"You see, Elliot," Zeek continued, "Since there is nothing that we have to do, and there are no absolute universal shoulds or oughts, the question then is 'what do you want to do?' Generally we are not ready for all this freedom. It results in a great deal of anxiety from the realization that one is truly accountable, and ultimately responsible for, one's own life.

"To avoid this reality a bird may engage in a frantic search for someone or something to tell him what to do; to sacrifice his freedom to avoid the anxiety in being responsible for his own life. A bird may choose to surrender his freedom to an institution, such as an eagle-order, or to a dogmatic system such as rigid flock law, or to another bird through a dependent relationship, surrendering one's freedom, so as to avoid the responsibility of making choices and commitments.

"Another way of shunning self-responsibility is to assume an 'ultimate rescuer'. This ultimate rescuer is generally viewed as a power that is outside of oneself, that adopts responsibility for us. This notion it is often employed to quell anxiety, with the hope for some form of intervention to tell us how to live, or what choices to make. These forms of responsibility avoidance tend to impair a bird's effectiveness, and to block mature functioning, which require the acceptance of self-responsibility.

"Understanding freedom helps us to deal with responsibility, Elliot, which involves decision making, choices and commitments. A decision is a very lonely act.

Decisions force us to accept personal responsibility, and confront us with anxiety though the realization that we are alone in the choice. It is our choice. A decision, and the resulting commitment, carries with it the connotation of finality. This is it... the impossibility of further possibility. That is the essence of what a decision involves; making a commitment which results in the impossibility of further possibility, the harsh reality that 'alternatives exclude'.

"Many times in flight we are faced with an A or B type choice, which can be very anxiety provoking. For then, we are committed to live with our choice, either A or B. As we fly down the course of life we encounter many 'forks' in the airways. We are repeatedly confronted with the alternatives of either taking the left or right path, with the resulting consequence of never knowing what 'might have been' down the other choice. Alternatives do exclude.

"These basic conditions of life, the dilemma of freedom and responsibility, the reality that alternatives often exclude in choices and commitments, cannot be avoided or totally overcome. Through acceptance of this limit-form, we can experience a liberating effect from the anxiety inherent in this predicament, thereby reducing our wasted time and energy in a futile attempt to overcome or avoid these conflicts and dilemmas."

Elliot was stunned at the truth in what Zeek said. No wonder making decisions is often so hard. It is a direct encounter with a limit, the limit of possibilities. To decide is to divide, to limit future opportunities. "Fascinating," he thought. "Such a subtle limit-form, yet one that all bird-beings wrestle with on a daily basis. Alternatives exclude."

Wings for Soaring - Part III

"And what of the other limit-form you mentioned?" Elliot inquired, eager to hear more.

"The second" Zeek began with a somber look on his face, "deals with changes and endings - the reality that everything fades. The experience of changes and endings in life is often very distressing. The myth of the contemporary eagle is that he's finally in control, that through knowledge, nature itself can be tamed and made a servant of The Great Council. Changes and endings confront this myth, and teach us that the universe is more vast than our ability to totally explain it. Few birds face or confront changes and endings freely by choice. Usually life experiences confront us, and these may include changes and endings in relationships, one's work, the loss of a loved one, or near death experiences through accidents or illnesses. If a bird is willing to face changes and endings, including his own mortality, instead of avoiding or denying them, many valuable lessons can be learned. A confrontation with a change or ending often results in major shifts in flight attitudes and behaviors. A bird can make quantum leaps in growth and development through facing this limit-form.

"One of these areas of growth often involves life perspectives and views. There is a realignment of life priorities, of what really matters, of what is important, of what is meaningful. Through facing changes and endings we learn that our unfinished business need not wait until we only have a few weeks, days, or hours to live. Life takes on a new sense of immediacy. We do not have time to waste. We cannot really count on tomorrow. Through facing one's finiteness, a bird can experience a sense of liberation from many of the shoulds and oughts. Many of the flock's customs and rituals are not nearly as binding, or as restrictive as they once were. Our incorporation of life's transitoriness enriches our life. It enables one to extricate himself from some of the smothering trivialities, to live more purposefully, more authentically, to be more open, honest, direct, and to assume more self-responsibility.

"Through confronting changes and endings, many eagles experience an enhanced sense of living in the present - here and now. The idea that each moment can be counted as a gift, one day at a time, one moment at a time. There is much less dwelling on the past or wishful thinking for the future.

"Another lesson that many learn is that they have an increased appreciation and delight in some of the subtle beauties of life, including nature, art, and relationships. Their senses seem to perk up. They tune into some of the subtlest little things. By being mindful of endings, one passes onto a state of gratitude, of appreciation for the countless joys of existence.

"Many also experience a deeper communication with loved ones, as a result of facing changes and endings. They start talking about things that matter, personal joys and concerns, hopes and dreams. There is a greater willingness to show caring and affection, more hugs, less small talk, less social chitchat and game playing. Eagles start relating as being to being, instead of playing games or remaining in rigid roles.

"A somewhat paradoxical result of confronting this limit-form is that many birds find that they have fewer fears in life. There is a greater willingness to take risks, a desire to live a full life, measured not by the clock and quantity, but by quality, the quality of one's existence. Birds are not so much afraid of their death, Elliot, as they are afraid of the incompleteness of their lives. An eagle who risks nothing, does nothing, has nothing, and is nothing. He may avoid suffering, pain, may postpone death, but he limits his capacity to learn, to grow, and to live. By facing this given, we find that we have fewer fears, and a greater willingness to take some of the risks that result in a fuller life.

"Erhart, one of my old instructors, spoke to me after he had a major structural failure in flight. He said the confrontation with death, and the reprieve from it, made everything look so precious, so sacred, so beautiful, that he felt more strongly than ever the impulse to love it, to embrace it, and to let himself be overwhelmed by it. Death and its present possibility, made love, passionate love, more possible. He wondered if we could love, if ecstasy would be possible at all, if we knew we would never die.

"Through facing this limit-form, each of us can feel less futile, less helpless, and less alone, even when ironically what we come to understand is the fact that each of us is basically alone and helpless in the face of universal indifference.

"Uncertainty exists in life, Elliot. There are no guarantees. Each of us needs to learn to co-exist with this uncertainty, to tolerate ambiguity, instead of frantically attempting to avoid or control these conditions."

Zeek paused for a moment. "Dealing with changes and endings is a letting-go process, Elliot. It is a skill that is needed and used throughout life. Through acceptance of change and ending as a part of life, including all the small mini-deaths that occur, there is a sense of peace and serenity. The saying 'Everything Fades' summarizes it well. Being mindful of this limit-form, and surrendering to it gracefully, can greatly enhance the joy and satisfaction one experiences in life. Acceptance helps to overcome the illusion that changes and endings can be avoided, ought to be fair and just, or must be controlled."

Again Elliot found Zeek's understanding and wisdom to have great clarity. The idea that 'everything fades' certainly rang true with his experience that change was perhaps the only permanent thing in life, and that many changes and endings in life seemed unfair and unjust.

Elliot and Zeek were silent for a while, as if all that was to be said, had been, and that no further explanation was necessary.

After some time Elliot spoke. "Thank you, Zeek. Your words have been useful to me in seeing more clearly these aspects of an eagle's lot."

Elliot felt a sense of contentment, as if he had come to terms with two more limit-forms. He decided to head south-east for a while to digest some of this new understanding, and perhaps do some soaring in the beautiful Wind River Range of mountains. After a good night's rest, Elliot bid Zeek good-bye, and headed south-easterly on a gentle climb out.

Wings for Soaring - Part IV

Around 10 o'clock thermals started popping near the Yellowstone Canyon, so Elliot started working the lift, looking for traces of wispy Cumulus clouds to mark the rising air currents. East of Buffalo Valley near Togwotee Pass, Elliot encountered some eerie smooth lift, up at about 200 feet-per-minute. He recognized it as the great mountain wave, and decided to work the powerful air current. Turning in to the westerly wind, Elliot hovered over Dubois, climbing upward through 20,000 feet near Gannett Peak in the Wind River mountain range.

From this peaceful space, Elliot began to reflect on the things he had talked about with Elizabeth and Zeek. His thoughts turned to the question of what it all might mean. What could be the purpose of his quest to understand limits?

Out of the corner of his eye, Elliot noticed another bird below him about 1500 feet, climbing up to his altitude. As the sunlight reflected off the silver-gray feathers of the visitor, Elliot maintained his position as the distinguished looking bird did an outside barrel roll around him, and then joined him in formation, inverted.

"Pretty view, isn't it?" commented Elliot's new wingman calmly.

"Why, yes," answered Elliot, somewhat taken aback by the gracefulness of this senior bird, "My name's Elliot."

"Nice to meet you Elliot, I'm Elijah."

Elliot remembered Zeek speaking about a master instructor of his named Elijah who taught Zeek about travel and compassion. He wondered. "You wouldn't happen to know Ezekiel, known as 'Zeek', would you?" he asked.

"I certainly do," replied Elijah, "Why, we flew together many flight-years ago. I remember him as being a very fast learner."

"Well, I feel as if I know you then." said Elliot. "Zeek was my flight instructor, and I've just come from talking with him."

"Oh yes," Elijah said smiling. "You must be the eager student that Zeek once spoke to me about, who tried to fly through granite."

Elliot realized he had a reputation for testing limits, but didn't know it had spread so widely. "Yes, I'm the one," he said reluctantly.

Elliot rolled inverted, staying in formation with Elijah, as they climbed up thru 30,000 feet.

"Have you ever wondered about life?" asked Elliot, testing this wise old bird's receptiveness to the question. "About what meaning and purpose there may be to one's existence."

"Yes," answered Elijah, sensing the seriousness of Elliot's question. "Why do you ask?"

Trying not to appear too eager, Elliot explained to Elijah his quest to understand all there is to know about limits, and his frustration in finding clear answers to questions of meaning and purpose.

"Elijah?" began Elliot rather hesitantly. "I would be interested in hearing your thoughts on life's meaning and purpose."

"I would be glad to share my understanding with you," responded Elijah, with a warm smile.

As the pair approached 40,000 feet Elijah began.

"As I've come to see it, Elliot, we as flight-beings tend to be creatures in search for meaning and purpose, and our airworthiness is dependent on the extent to which we are able to experience a sense of meaning and purpose in life. The contemporary bird's dilemma is that he is not told by instincts what he must do, or by waning flock traditions what he should do, and oftentimes he does not know what it is he wants to do. Many birds have difficulty in finding meaning and purpose in life.

"When there is a distinct life vacuum, a lack of meaning, symptoms often rush in to fill it. These symptoms include obsessive-compulsive behaviors such as overeating, reckless flying, and depression. They can also include a variety of delinquent or flock defiant acts. These are often desperate attempts to fill the void, to overcome the sense of meaninglessness. Having time on one's wings can be problematic because it confronts one with the question of what to do with the time. What is meaningful? What should I do? What do I really want to do with my life?

"The issue of life's meaning and purpose is one that has been wrestled with throughout all of recorded history, Elliot. As flight-beings, we have the capacity to be self-aware, to step outside of ourselves, to assume a detached view. This capacity for self-awareness and self-detachment can be very valuable and therapeutic. It also has some risks, however. There is a danger.

"There are some problems which occur when we step back too far, or when we stay there too long. When we assume a high altitude view, or aloof perspective of life, we can get into trouble. This detached viewpoint tends to drain vitality from life. To assume it for a prolonged period of time can result in a sense of despair that nothing matters, and continued immersion in a lofty viewpoint may be lethal. It can result in severe depression and suicidal thoughts. There is a saying that sums it up quite well; 'Analysis leads to paralysis'. If we are very busy analyzing life, asking all sorts of 'Why?' or 'What for?' questions, we tend to get paralyzed. We are impaired. Our ability to engage in life, to fully participate, is blocked.

"The direct quest for the ultimate meaning of life can be a self-sabotaging endeavor. The search for life meaning is paradoxical in that the more we search for it, the less we find it. A frantic search for the 'goal' or 'point' of life can lead to a sense of meaninglessness and despair, that nothing matters from a high altitude, or cosmic viewpoint.

"The answer, a sense of meaning and purpose in life, is found by looking away from the question, by disengaging from the detached viewpoint, and by engaging in life. Life is a gift, Elliot. Take it, unwrap it, appreciate it, use it, and enjoy it."

"Regardless of one's religious beliefs, philosophical views, or scientific approach to life, all beings are confronted with the same basic challenge of finding meaning and purpose in life. Although half-sure, we can whole-heartedly leap into engagement. To gracefully immerse oneself in the airwaves of life. To be fully present, here and now. To get into being."

Elijah paused for a few moments. After completing a slow roll he continued.

"There are three primary flight paths to meaning," Elijah went on to explain. "One is through creativity. Creativity in what we do, what we give to the world, in how we use our time and energy. This could include artistic aerobatics, flight instruction, and truth discovery. To create or discover something new, to put something together in a different way, something of beauty, something of harmony. As for the question of 'Why?' or 'What for?', for its own sake, it really needs no excuse or reason. Creativity is intrinsically rewarding and satisfying in and of itself. The creative process of using our time and energy results in joy and well-being. It is meaningful.

"A second way to meaning is through experiences that we have, what we take in, what we get from the world. Through experiencing truth, beauty, the love of another being, we experience a sense of meaning and purpose in life. Tuning into the natural order around us, sensing the subtle and delicate balances in life, joining the harmony which exists, being aware of it, appreciating it, and delighting in it, results in a meaningful existence.

"A third means centers on our flight attitude in life. An attitude that tends to focus on 'what is not' or 'what cannot be', results in a great deal of frustration and disappointment. In contrast, by focusing on 'what is' and 'what can be', life meaning and purpose looms. Meaning potentials and opportunities take form, and give us direction and purpose in flight.

"You see, Elliot, ironically by not getting caught up in the notion that one should or must have an answer to the question of 'What's the meaning of life?', one is freer to experience a sense of meaning and purpose in life, through passionate engagement, by doing and experiencing what is, and what can be."

"Analysis leads to paralysis..." thought Elliot. Boy, did that ever hit home. All too often had he been paralyzed by his hyper-active mind. Indeed, "I think I think too much!!" he thought to himself, with a chuckle.

Elliot was beginning to see how one could experience a sense of meaning and purpose in life, in spite of not having definitive answers to questions about the meaning of life. This intellectual limit-form did not necessarily limit one's freedom to experience things that matter.

Not feeling a need to say anything, Elliot nodded to Elijah, indicating he had grasped the essence of what was said. With that, Elijah completed a gentle wing-over followed by a Split-S, leaving as gracefully as he had arrived.

Epilogue

On his flight back home, Elliot caught some more wave lift near Hoback Junction. He worked the lift up to 50,000 feet, and enjoyed the spectacular view. Elliot's mind began to wander again, high aloft, pondering such things as previous lives, beyond death, and cosmic purpose. He became so consumed by his mental ramblings that he failed to notice the beautiful sunset over the Grand Tetons.

Suddenly, a blazing thought-realization occurred to Elliot. "Here and now's the place to be, this is it, all you see!!!"

Startled, as if awakened from a dream, Elliot almost stalled as he realized the potentials of this perspective. At first the idea was shocking, because it flew in the face of so many teachings which tend to focus on the future, and alternate realities. In time, however, he found that this way of being had a liberating effect, freeing him from much of his wishful thinking. "This Is It - Here & Now," he thought, "Far Out!!!"

As Elliot made his approach home passing over the Gros Ventre River, he felt more totally present and aware of life than ever before. Elliot had accepted life's terms. He was beginning to understand the paradox of how he could have total freedom, within absolute limits. Unencumbered by myths, illusions and fantasies, he was free to delight in just being, without expecting anything else - free to enjoy his *wings for soaring*.

****

<u>*Addendum*</u>

"Wings Of Wisdom"

Uplifting Essence Essays

By Psychologist

"Dr. Dan" Matzke, PhD

On Life & Living
Seven Golden Guidelines

On Personal Effectiveness
Seven Powerful Pointers

On The Art & Technique Of
Mindfulness

On Great Insights & Ideas
Of Humanity

On Life & Living
Seven Golden Guidelines

By Psychologist "Dr. Dan" Matzke, PhD

Truth
Seek truth, truthfulness and genuineness.
Be real, honest and sincere,
And seek others who are authentic.

Beauty
Look for beauty and good in nature, art and people.
Appreciate aesthetic magnificence and grandeur.

Excellence
Strive for excellence and quality in all endeavors.
Enjoy the elements of grace and elegance.

Wisdom
Seek wisdom and the prudent use of knowledge.
Aim to use good reasoning and judgment.

Justice
Strive for justice, fairness and reasonableness.
Be compassionate and caring with integrity.

Courage
Have the courage to stand for that which is best.
Be courageous with valor and gallantry.

Moderation
Seek balance and harmony in life.
Exercise moderation and temperance in living.

Author's Note: The above thoughts, ideas and perspectives are drawn from great seminal thinkers throughout all of recorded history. These are wise time-tested principles which can be powerful tools - useful in guiding one's daily actions toward life success and happiness. Interested readers are referred to classical writings in literature, philosophy and spirituality for further study. Other programs and books by Dr. Dan are available at *UpliftingPerspectives.net* PS – You are invited to share this essay.

>>>>>>><<<<<<<

On Personal Effectiveness
Seven Powerful Pointers

By Psychologist "Dr. Dan" Matzke, PhD

Planning
Think ahead - be proactive.
Prioritize and organize future actions.

Preparedness
Aim for anticipation and prevention.
Strive to be ready for future needs.

Pacing
Aspire for flow without force.
Adjust the pace to fit the place.

Persistence
Endeavor for progress and progression.
Take the steps one at a time.

Perspective
For best perspective - be objective.
Seek to see the big picture.

Patience
Be here – now.
Question the need to hurry or rush.

Personal-Responsibility
Focus on choices and commitments.
Get real... Get a grip... Get on with it.

Author's Note: While the above pointers are basic and primary, they are critical and essential for personal effectiveness. The guideposts can also point to matters that one is ignoring or avoiding (due to fear, dread, etc.) which are road blocks and barriers towards the next step and/or the next level in one's endeavors and life journey. A good "rule of thumb" is that ten percent (10%) extra effort invested in using these principles results in a ninety percent (90%) difference. Developing one's awareness of and practicing these pointers and self-coaching tools can yield significant benefits – enabling one to "take a hold of life" and face challenges with courage and confidence. Other programs and books by Dr. Dan are available at *UpliftingPerspectives.net* PS - You are invited to share this essay.

>>>>>>><<<<<<<

On The Art & Technique Of
Mindfulness

Powerful Principles & Practices
For Personal Growth & Development
Peak Performance & Well-Being

By Psychologist "Dr. Dan" Matzke, PhD

This essence essay considers the art and technique of mindfulness – which can be described as a mental state of clear minded awareness that is unencumbered, unfettered and unhurried. The art of mindfulness entails being fully present to experience and savor being alive, awake and aware. The technique of mindfulness involves consciously focusing one's attention on thoughts, feelings and actions, many of which can at times be self-defeating and toxic. Three core issues can be identified which often overlap and interact with each other, much like the strands of a rope. These are natural tendencies and habit patterns which all human beings struggle with:

Keep Critical, Judgmental & Negative Thinking
In Check

Nurture
Positive Perspectives

Temper Unfounded
Fears & Self-Doubts

Develop A
Trusting Attitude

Be Cautious Of Consumption By
The Past & The Future

Practice Being Present
Here & Now

Author's Note: The above principles of mindfulness are time-tested realistic practices, which were first articulated over 2500 years ago. These ideas are powerful pointers and skills which can greatly enhance personal effectiveness and well-being. Other programs and books by Dr. Dan are available at *UpliftingPerspectives.net* PS - You are invited to share this essay.

On Great Insights & Ideas Of Humanity

By Psychologist "Dr. Dan" Matzke, PhD

This essence essay explores great insights and ideas of humanity, timeless penetrating perspectives on the nature of being and reality – which have been discovered and re-discovered by seminal thinkers, teachers and open-minded individuals in the East and West, throughout all of recorded history. The work endeavors to distill the inherent universal wisdom into uplifting statements, which can be useful in life and living. These primary concepts often overlap and interact with each other, much like the strands of a rope:

*

Truth, beauty, joy and peace are readily available in life, here and now. There is no special place to go, and nothing out of the ordinary to do, to acquire access to these merits – other than to "get real", "come to your senses", and "pay attention".

**

Mindfulness of the awe, wonder and mystery - in life, nature and the universe - leaves one humbly standing with reverence and gratitude for being. Trusting the intrinsic power and wisdom that is experienced in life yields peace and serenity.

***

Realization of universal oneness and unity leads to understanding and compassion. Estrangement and alienation from one's own self, others and the world leads to discord and destructiveness.

****

Preoccupation and consumption by the past and the future (e.g. drivenness and hurry sickness) are human foibles that rob one of being fully present to savor and participate in life. Realization of the ultimate magnitude of the moment enhances enjoyment and effectiveness.

*****

Direct experience is the primary pathway to realization. While teachings, writings and prescribed practices can "point the way" – they are not equivalent to actual personal experience – and they may interfere with the learning and growth process.

******

Much of our understanding, and many of our experiences, are at a level which is beyond the intellect's abilities to explain or to communicate (ranging from simple experiences like riding a bike and swimming - to profound insight into the nature of being and reality). This deeply innate, intuitive "knowing" is often overlooked, undervalued and doubted – yet it is far more crucial and powerful than our limited mental and verbal abilities.

****

Comprehending the true nature of being entails courageously facing reality, seeing clearly how it is, and "coming to terms" with life and living. By recognizing and resolving disquieting matters, and life's ultimate concerns, one is able to live more fully and richly – having the presence to savor being alive, awake and aware.

Author's Note:

The above universal self-evident truths are time-tested and realistic. These are powerful insights and ideas which can greatly enhance personal effectiveness and well-being. The reader is kindly encouraged to sincerely and courageously seek understanding – to see the true nature of being and reality. Other articles and books by Dr. Dan are available at *UpliftingPerspectives.net* PS - You are invited to share this essay.

Printed in Great Britain
by Amazon